Animated Films

RHODA NOTTRIDGE

Crestwood House
New York

Titles in this series

Adventure Films
Animated Films
Horror Films
Science Fiction Films

Words in **bold** appear in the glossary.

Cover: An American Tail TM (1986) was one of the few full-animation films made in recent years.

Series Editor: Deborah Elliott
Book Editor: Geraldine Purcell
Designer: Helen White

First Crestwood House edition 1992
© Copyright 1991 by Wayland (Publishers) Limited

Crestwood House
Macmillan Publishing Company
866 Third Avenue
New York, NY 10022

Macmillan Publishing Company is part of the Maxwell Communication Group of Companies.

First published in 1991 by Wayland (Publishers) Limited
61 Western Road, Hove, East Sussex, England BN3 1JD

Library of Congress Cataloging-in-Publication Data
 Nottridge, Rhoda.
  Animated films/Rhoda Nottridge.
    p.   cm. — (Films)
  Includes bibliographical references and index.
  Summary: Surveys the field of animated films, from the early cartoons to the European scene, computerized cartoons, and contemporary examples.
   ISBN 0-89686-717-X
   1. Animated films—Juvenile literature. [1. Animated films.]
 I. Title. II. Series: Films (Crestwood House)
 NC1765.N68   1992
 791.43'3—dc20   91-36041
                                                  CIP
                                                   AC

Printed by G. Canale C.S.p.A., Turin, Italy

1 2 3 4 5 6 7 8 9 10

Contents

Moving pictures

ABOVE **Winsor McCay created his charming and very popular character Gertie the Dinosaur with simple line drawings.**

MOVING pictures appear to have fascinated many inventors in the nineteenth century. Machines with strange names, such as the Zoetrope and Praxinoscope, were created. These made a series of images appear to move.

As filmmaking and photography developed at the beginning of this century, **illustrators** and **cartoonists** began to realize their importance. With moving pictures they would be able to bring pictures and characters to life!

Emile Cohl, a French illustrator, made the first animated film in 1908. It was called *Fantasmagorie* and lasted for only two minutes. In the United States, **comic strip** artist Winsor McCay used his simple style of drawing to make cartoon films such as *Gertie the Dinosaur* (1909).

His work was an immediate success. At this time, many Europeans who had moved to the United States felt isolated because they did not speak English. McCay's simple and moving cartoon stories did not use words. Sound had yet to be developed in filmmaking, so cartoons were films that anyone could understand because the stories were told through pictures. Even today some cartoons are made that do not use spoken language.

To make animated films, a series of still pictures flash before the audience's eyes so quickly that the images appear to be moving. An animated film is actually made up of thousands of pictures.

In the early days of animated films, illustrators had to draw every single movement in a new picture. All of the pictures were then photographed one after another onto a **reel** of film. Drawing the pictures took a long time. That is why the comic strip style of many cartoons developed. The simpler the style of drawing, as in cartoon pictures, the easier it was to make large numbers of pictures.

The heavy workload of the illustrators was changed by the introduction of "cel" **animation**. The drawings were put on clear sheets of film, called celluloid. One image could be put on top of

BELOW **This cel drawing from** *Scrooge* **was placed on top of the background drawing (below left) and then photographed to make just one of the many thousands of stills that make up the film.**

another. This meant that fewer drawings were needed. For example, if a dog wagged its tail, one drawing of the main body of the dog could be made. Separate drawings on celluloid, of the tail moving, would be laid over the picture of the rest of the dog. In this way the whole dog would not have to be redrawn for each movement.

Cel animation encouraged many illustrators to move into making animated films. Large American film companies, such as Paramount and Metro-Goldwyn-Mayer (MGM), set up **studios** for the illustrators to work in.

BELOW **Don Bluth, the creator of** *An American Tail*™ **(1986), drawing one of the main characters onto a cel.**

Early cartoon stars

BY 1919, Felix the Cat, created by Otto Messmer, was launched as a cartoon character. The idea of Felix came from a Rudyard Kipling story called *The Cat that Walked by Himself*. The Felix films were very popular. Felix was the first cartoon animal to become as famous as a human movie star. Felix the Cat later went on to make a number of television appearances in the 1930s.

ABOVE **Felix the Cat was a funny, naughty and lovable character who was popular with audiences around the world during the 1920s and 1930s.**

Koko the Clown, a character who comes to life out of an **inkwell**, was another cartoon character in the 1920s. His creator, Max Fleischer, and his studio team went on to produce characters such as Betty Boop (a cartoon Hollywood starlet) in 1932 and Popeye in 1933.

Woody Woodpecker was created by the famous Walter Lantz in the 1940s. Lantz also worked at Fleischer's studio. Woody was based on a real woodpecker who continually annoyed Lantz when he was on his honeymoon. His wife suggested he draw some cartoons of the bird to help him forget about its noisy pecking. Instead of being forgotten, the woodpecker was turned into the hilarious character of Woody. Lantz's wife actually played Woody's voice in the cartoons.

The large American studios brought together many talented cartoonists, such as Lantz and

Tex Avery. Another young artist named Chuck Jones learned how to work on cartoon films from animators at the Warner Brothers Studios. As a child, Chuck Jones lived next door to Charlie Chaplin's studio. (Chaplin was a famous comedy actor in silent films.) From watching Chaplin, Jones learned a lot about action and timing in comedy. When he became a cartoon artist, or animator, this sense of timing helped him a lot. Jones went on to help create popular cartoon characters such as Bugs Bunny, Porky Pig, Pepe le Pew and Daffy Duck.

Bugs Bunny actually began life as a hare in *Porky's Hare Hunt* (1938). He was changed into a smart rabbit for later films.

OPPOSITE **Max Fleischer's character Betty Boop, the Hollywood starlet, was popular in the 1930s.**

BELOW **In 1928 Walt Disney created one of the best-loved and longest-lasting animated characters, Mickey Mouse.**

Disney's cartoon world

ABOVE **Walt Disney, pictured with some of the many Academy Awards that Disney movies have won.**

WALT Disney was a young American artist. He created a character called Oswald the Lucky Rabbit for Universal Studios. The Oswald character was very popular and earned the company a great deal of money. Although Disney had created Oswald, Universal insisted that they owned the **copyright** to the character. Disney left Universal in disgust and decided to set up his own company in Hollywood.

In 1928, Walt Disney was **doodling** during a train ride. He came up with an unlikely cartoon character called Mortimer Mouse. The mouse's name was later changed to Mickey. Mickey Mouse was to become Disney's most famous doodle.

Disney asked his friend Ub Iwerks to produce 700 drawings a day to make the first animated film starring Mickey Mouse, called *Plane Crazy* (1928). Not everyone liked the character. Louis B. Mayer of MGM Studios refused to give Disney any promises of work because he thought that pregnant women would be frightened by a huge mouse appearing in the film!

Disney did not drop Mickey. Instead, he let him star in *Steamboat Willie* (1928). As sound had now been developed for films, animated films were no longer silent. Disney honored his little mouse character by playing Mickey's voice himself in the first-ever cartoon with speech.

Mickey Mouse shot to stardom. By 1934 he received more fan mail than any other Hollywood star. This is perhaps surprising for a star who is actually just a series of drawings, rather than a real person.

Disney was not slow to see Mickey Mouse's potential. He created a friend for Mickey, named Minnie Mouse, and a dog named Pluto. In the 1930s a total of 87 films featuring Mickey Mouse were made. In just one year, about 468 million people saw Mickey Mouse on film.

A Mickey Mouse Club was started by Disney and eventually had over a million members. Disney was one of the first film-makers to realize that he could use his films to sell lots of goods. One of his first ideas was to produce 30 million Mickey Mouse-shaped ice-cream cones. Hundreds of other products followed. In just one day, 11,000 Mickey Mouse watches were sold in a New York department store. To this day, a wide range of Mickey Mouse products is sold all over the world.

BELOW **A big attraction for visitors to Disney World in Florida is the chance to see their favorite cartoon characters, such as Mickey Mouse and Goofy.**

The first cartoon feature

BELOW **Audiences loved Disney's charming and beautifully drawn cartoon version of the famous fairy tale** *Snow White and the Seven Dwarfs* **(1937).**

DISNEY'S success with Mickey Mouse might have seemed enough for one lifetime, but he was already working on many new ideas. Delving back into fairy tales, Disney came across *Snow White and the Seven Dwarfs*. It was to be the first American full-length cartoon feature film. It was also the world's first cartoon film to have sound and be in color.

Making a feature-length film required more than just putting together lots of short films. In *Snow White and the Seven Dwarfs* (1937), it was necessary

HIS FIRST FULL LENGTH FEATURE PRODUCTION!

Walt **DISNEY'S** **Snow White** *in the Marvelous* **MULTIPLANE TECHNICOLOR**

and the Seven Dwarfs

©WDP

"Grumpy, let me see YOUR hands!"

to keep the audience's attention for 87 minutes, not the usual 8 minutes that animated films had previously lasted. Disney and his animators studied live-action films, theater and even ballet to see how they kept the audience interested. In a short cartoon film the pace is fast, with lots of action. In a full-length film, there has to be a good story that involves the audience and builds up to a dramatic ending.

Snow White and the Seven Dwarfs was an ambitious project in other ways too. The animators had to draw a convincing human figure for Snow White, although they had been used to drawing only overgrown mice and ducks. Thousands of drawings were sketched to try to get the characters right before the final film drawings were made.

ABOVE **Actors dressed as Snow White and one of the dwarfs, Dopey, amuse an audience at Disney World.**

Disney used 300 artists, who worked in teams for twenty-four hours a day, seven days a week, for over six months. Disney had been planning the film since 1933. It was finally shown in 1937, having cost six times more to make than he had thought it would.

Snow White and the Seven Dwarfs was an immediate success. Disney believed that the film appealed to both adults and children because it took the viewers back to the simple, unspoiled kind of world that we can all remember from childhood stories.

Behind the scenes

YOUR SYNOPSIS
The Adventures of a toy that becomes a boy.

ABOVE *Pinocchio* **(1940) told the story of a little wooden toy that wanted to be a real-life boy. Walt Disney's attention to detail and the mixture of an amusing story and wonderful songs has made** *Pinocchio* **one of the most popular Disney feature films.**

DISNEY'S success seemed endless. From 1931 on, he won every **Academy Award** for animation for eleven years. After *Snow White and the Seven Dwarfs*, *Pinocchio* (1940) and *Bambi* (1942) were his next two **classics**.

Disney was a great believer in research for his films. This may have been what put him ahead of other American animation studios. He knew how important it was to know about different types of art. Animators working on Mickey Mouse were sent off to **life-drawing** classes so that they could study human figures and movements. These art lessons helped them improve the characters.

Sound was also an important influence. In *Pinocchio* Disney developed the character of the cricket. This creature had a small part in the original nineteenth-century story by Carlo Collodi (which Disney had borrowed from for the film). At first Disney made Jiminy Cricket a stuffy and boastful little creature. He gave the voice and singing part of Jiminy to an entertainer named Cliff Edwards. When Edwards sang "When You Wish Upon a Star," the character of Jiminy seemed merrier and more fun than Disney's original drawings of him. So Disney set to work on changing Jiminy's appearance, to fit the voice Edwards had given to the little talking cricket.

Disney believed that his animators needed to look at the world around them to fire their imaginations and create the best cartoons. For the underwater scenes in *Pinocchio* he sent his artists out to film and sketch the sea and the coastline. They collected shells and studied the wonders of the sea world through glass-bottomed boats.

Disney then went even further into making cartoons from real life with *Bambi* — the story of a wild fawn. A live deer was brought into the studios for the artists to work from. Special films were made of the changing seasons in a woods for the artists to study, so they could appreciate the atmosphere of a forest. Rabbits, mice, skunks and other creatures were brought in so that the animators could observe all their movements. These creatures became the screen character friends of Bambi — Thumper (the rabbit) and Flower (the skunk).

BELOW **Many Disney feature films have been released on videocassettes so that people can buy or rent their favorites.**

Bambi paved the way for other **sentimental** films that had popular appeal. In these animated films all the characters had problems that filled the audience with sympathy. For example, Bambi feared losing his mother. In 1941, *Dumbo* had already left audiences crying because he was a baby elephant who was laughed at for having outsized ears. However, the audiences would cheer when he ended up as a national celebrity in the film. Disney had mastered the art of pulling the heartstrings of his audience with his little cartoon characters.

The European scene

DISNEY and the American animators led the world in the type of films whose origins were based in comic strips. Other types of animation developed in a very different way in Europe and the rest of the world.

Since the early days of filmmaking, artists had experimented with other animation methods. As well as cartoon drawings, puppets and cutout shapes were animated to make short films.

The very first animated film did in fact come from the United States. In 1898 Albert Smith borrowed his daughter's toy circus and brought it to life! He filmed the acrobats and animals, moving them very slightly from shot to shot, so that when the whole film was played they appeared to move.

In Britain, *Noah's Ark* (1908) and *Dreams of Toyland* (1908) by Arthur Melbourne Cooper used the same method to bring toys to life. While the animation and cartoon industry grew and grew in the United States, very little happened in Europe. World War I had started in 1914, and there was no time or money to develop such an industry. By the time the war was over, Americans had already begun to set up cartoon studios attached to film companies. They had the **facilities** and the money to perfect their cartoons. Europe could not compete. American animated films dominated the European movie theaters.

In the USSR, animation was developing separately. The Soviets had a wealth of beautiful folk stories, and puppet theaters were popular.

LEFT **A scene from one of Ladislas Starevitch's early puppet-animation films.**

Animated puppet films soon became just as popular. The Soviet animator Ladislas Starevitch moved to Paris, bringing the puppet tradition with him. He produced charming films, such as *The Voice of the Nightingale* (1923).

Animation in the USSR was also used for news films. *Soviet Toys* (1924) by Dziga Vertov is one example. This type of film used the Soviet tradition of **satirical** illustrations to show how awful life was for poor people in the USSR. Vertov's film was partly made of cutout pictures. The technique involves cutting out paper shapes and then moving them slightly for each shot.

The Adventures of Prince Achmed (1926) is probably the finest example of the cutout technique of animation. Lotte Reiniger, from Germany, created extraordinary and powerful scenes using this method. The cartoon style of American films at this time did not achieve the beautiful detail that could be created with cutouts.

OPPOSITE **A series of stills from Lotte Reiniger's *The Frog Prince*, which was made using the cutout technique.**

North American revival

THE growth of television in the 1950s gave the animated film industry a much wider audience, particularly in the United States.

Disney Studios, United Productions of America (UPA), MGM and Warner Brothers thrived on the comic-style cartoons. UPA was set up in the 1940s by a group of employees who had left the Disney Studios. They avoided the sentimental, fairy-tale style of Disney films by creating characters who lived in a dangerous and cruel world.

Disney was still interested in fantasy tales. He made *Cinderella*, *Peter Pan* and *Alice in Wonderland* in the 1950s. In 1966, Walt Disney died, but his huge business empire continues with many films and the Disneyland and Disney World theme parks. *The Jungle Book* (1967), released a year after his death, is considered by some to be Disney's finest work.

Some of the younger animators who had been working in Europe moved to North America where there were more facilities and more money. They brought fresh influences to the world of animation. Oskar Fischinger, Norman McLaren and Len Lye, a New Zealander, were all interested in experimenting with animation and came up with unusual ideas and approaches.

The money used to make these experimental films often came from arts funds rather than cartoon studios. The National Film Board of Canada attracted animators from around the world by paying for unusual new films. Animators such as Norman McLaren could develop unique styles of working. Canada's reputation as a producer of an enormous variety of excellent animated films remains to this day.

The work of Caroline Leaf is a good example of the sponsorship of the National Film Board of Canada. Leaf came up with a form of animation called sand-cel. She created pictures out of sand by changing the image for each shot of the film with her fingers. This made the sand image come to life. Leaf and an **Inuit** artist named Nanogak worked together on an animated sand-cel film of an Inuit **legend**. It took a year and a half to make the film.

Caroline Leaf has since gone on to produce the award-winning *The Street* (1976). She finger-painted onto glass, changing the position of the ink slightly for each picture in order to make the characters move.

LEFT **Animators are always looking for new ways to animate stories on film. Caroline Leaf's finger-painting technique used in** *The Street* **(1976) suggests that the possibilities are endless.**

Animation in the Far East

ABOVE **Japan's Kihachiro Kawamoto, who made** *Demon* **(1972), is considered by many to be a master of puppet animation.**

THE Chinese film industry started in the Shanghai Studios in the 1920s. Like the Americans, they adopted the cartoon style. The first Chinese animated film, *Camel's Dance*, appeared in the 1930s.

The Chinese film industry went into decline but made a comeback in the 1950s. The Chinese used figures and styles that were special to their country and its history. The figure of the Monkey King, taken from Chinese legends, became popular. He first appeared in *Havoc in Heaven*, made by Wan Lai-Ming. The Chinese originally preferred to use cutout pictures for their cartoons but have slowly moved on to other techniques.

In Japan, the film industry grew rapidly after the end of World War II, producing comic-strip-style cartoons. However, by the 1960s, artists such as Yoji Kuri developed new styles of line-drawing cartoons.

More recently, Kihachiro Kawamoto has drawn on Japanese folktales and puppetry to produce masterpieces such as *Demon* (1972).

The Japanese animation industry now employs about 25,000 people. As well as encouraging more unusual forms of animation, Japan produces the largest number of animated television programs in the world for children.

Animation in Britain

IN 1954 two British illustrators, John Halas and Joy Batchelor, decided to tackle the idea of making an animated film about a serious story. They chose the George Orwell novel *Animal Farm*. The story is a clever tale of how the animals on a farm stage a **revolution**. The film is unsentimental, even though it features cartoon-style animals.

Animal Farm was the first British feature-length cartoon film. It further developed the idea of using animated films to be both serious and educational.

This idea of a serious cartoon film was used in an adaptation of Raymond Briggs's story *When the Wind Blows* (1986), about the terrible effects of nuclear weapons.

In a more lighthearted and touching vein, another of Raymond Briggs's fantasy stories, *The Snowman*, was made into a beautifully animated short film for television in 1985.

ABOVE **A scene from the "serious" cartoon film *Animal Farm* (1954), which broke away from the idea that animated films are only a form of light entertainment.**

BELOW In *Creature Comforts* **(1990) the animal models "talked" about life in a zoo.**

British cartoon and animation techniques are continually developing. The British animator Nick Park won the 1991 Academy Award for the best animated film, *Creature Comforts* (1990), which used plastic models of animals in a zoo.

USSR & Eastern Europe

ANIMATION in the USSR has developed using many individual styles. The animation industry was particularly strong in the 1930s. The Soviet state funded many animators whose work was aimed at putting across moral values to children. However, there has also been a steady stream of animated films for adults, which have quietly criticized the government of the USSR. Other types of films and literature have sometimes been banned in the country, but animators have managed to make films that challenge values in their society. This is generally because their films also contain humor and a good story.

Ivan Ivanov-Vano has been called the Soviet Walt Disney. Like Disney, he is a cartoonist who enthralls his audiences. Ivanov-Vano's stories are influenced by Soviet poetry, art, embroidery and carving, as well as traditional folktales. His finely detailed and colorful masterpieces include *The Tale of a Dead Princess* (1953) and *The Magic Lake* (1979). Ivanov-Vano has been an inspiration to many young Soviet animators, such as Yuri Norstein.

Today, animation is blossoming in the smaller republics of the USSR. These republics have developed their own styles, based on their local culture. For example, there are **Oriental** influences to be seen in the work of animators living in the eastern and southern states of the USSR.

Many East European countries, such as Poland, Czechoslovakia and Hungary, also have their own individual styles of animation. These styles have

ABOVE **This scene from Ivan Ivanov-Vano's** *The Magic Lake* **(1979) shows how beautifully drawn and detailed his films are.**

developed to some extent separately from the rest of the world. This has meant that animators have created new and exciting films influenced by the art and culture of their countries.

One of the great features of animated films is that they have developed in so many different ways in so many different countries. What is marvelous is that these films do not depend on words. They can communicate feelings and thoughts that can be understood by people all over the world.

Computerized cartoons

THERE will always be a place for the lovingly hand-drawn, unique and experimental types of animated films. One of the joys of animated films is that anyone can make them. All that is required is access to a film camera and lots of imagination and patience.

Now, however, the large animation studios around the world are using increasingly sophisticated technology to aid animation. Working first with simple patterns, computer experts began to see how artists could use computer programs. *Lapis*, created by James Whitney, was one of the first experimental films in this field.

The development of computer-aided animation was a slow process. The new technology was being designed by scientists, who could not always understand what artists could and could not do.

At first, computer-aided animation was used only for scientific purposes, such as creating television weather forecast maps that shifted patterns to show weather changes.

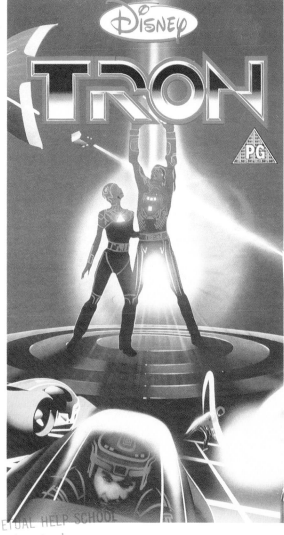

BELOW **The Disney film** *Tron* **(1982) uses actors and computer-aided animation.**

25

One of the great advances in computer-aided animation was the development of **light pens** and **electronic drawing pads**. The artist "draws" with the pen onto a pad, which remembers the picture. The artist can then command the computer to change the image in a number of ways, one of which is to make the image move, therefore animating it.

Computer-aided animation can also make images appear to be **three-dimensional**. Three-dimensional animation is often used today, especially in television, advertisements and rock videos. The first three-dimensional, full-length animated film was *Abracadabra* (1982), an Australian science-fiction musical. *The Adventures of André and Wally B* (1984) is also a good early example of this kind of film. The cartoon characters came to life, appearing as solid, rounded creatures.

There have been many other breakthroughs in animation. For example, a photographic image can be changed and made to "move." This makes it very difficult to know whether an image we are looking at is "real" or made by a computer with human help.

RIGHT **A scene from the three-dimensional, computer-animated film** *The Adventures of André and Wally B* **(1984).**

Cartoons today

FILMS, television commercials and rock videos often combine animated scenes with live action. *Who Framed Roger Rabbit?* (1988) was very successful because of its clever and amusing mix of human and cartoon characters.

Actor Bob Hoskins plays a private detective, in the well-established film style of the 1930s, struggling to make a living. His client is a rather comical, worried, cartoon film star, Roger Rabbit. He is being hunted down for a crime that he did

ABOVE **The mixing of real-life actors and cartoon characters proved to be a huge success in** *Who Framed Roger Rabbit?* **(1988).**

OPPOSITE
Originally the Teenage Mutant Ninja Turtles were cartoon characters created for television.

not commit. To discover more about the situation, Bob Hoskins enters "Toonland" – a magical world peopled entirely by cartoon characters.

To have real humans acting with cartoons is always tricky. It meant that during the filming Hoskins was actually pretending to talk to characters who did not exist. He had to know exactly where the cartoon characters would appear in the film and direct his speech and positioning toward them, even though there was not actually anyone standing there. The cartoons were added to the film later.

Who Framed Roger Rabbit? also owes much to the Tom-and-Jerry-style films. Characters get squashed, squeezed and spun and yet bounce back to life. The film is slightly different, though, because we all know that the humans will not survive the kind of blows that cartoon characters can deal out and receive.

There is a sense that the animated characters are out of control. This may say something about cartoon creatures in the film industry today. There are now thousands of cartoon characters, although new ones, such as the Teenage Mutant Ninja Turtles, tend to be created for television,

Around the world, cartoon characters continue to be loved by both adults and children. However, the little cartoon creatures had better watch out. There are lots of new, different characters coming to life – from the sand creatures of Caroline Leaf to the creations made using computerized techniques employed by large studios. Animators are continually finding new ways to tell sad, funny and serious stories through various techniques and different characters to audiences around the world.

Glossary

Academy Award An award given by the American film industry to
people who contribute in some major way to the making of a film.
Animation The process of making a still object or drawing move or
appear to move.
Cartoonists Artists who work in a quick style that is often used for
comic strips or stories.
Classics Books and films that are considered to be of a very high
standard.
Comic strip A series of cartoon pictures, sometimes with words,
which tell a story that is often funny.
Copyright The legal right to use, and control the use of, a piece of
literature, music or art, such as a cartoon character.
Doodling Idly drawing without any real reason for doing so.
Electronic drawing pad A pad with electronic sensors that can pick
up the signals from a light pen and show them as lines or marks
on a computer's display screen.
Facilities The buildings and equipment that make a job possible or
easier.
Illustrators Artists who paint pictures that decorate or explain
something.
Inkwell A pot in which ink is kept for use with a fountain pen.
Inuit The native tribespeople who live in the areas north of the Arctic
Circle (near the North Pole).
Legend A story that has been retold for many years or centuries.
Life drawing Drawing that is done from real life, where a real object
or person is there for an artist to look at.
Light pen A penlike object that, when used on an electronic drawing
pad, can send signals that make lines and marks appear on a
computer's display screen.
Oriental Coming from the Orient, or Far East.
Reel A spool that has a length of photographic film wound around it.

Revolution   An organized uprising, or revolt, usually against a
   country's government or the people who rule it.
Satirical   A kind of sharp humor that makes a serious point.
Sentimental   Overly emotional.
Studios   Places where artists, filmmakers or other people in the film
   industry work.
Three-dimensional   All solid objects are three-dimensional – that is,
   they can be viewed from all sides. Drawings are flat and therefore
   are two-dimensional, but artists can use clever techniques to give
   the impression that the drawn objects are solid.

Further reading

Belgrano, Giovanni. *Let's Make a Movie.* New York: Scroll Press, 1973.

Cohen, Daniel. *Masters of Horror.* Boston: Houghton Mifflin, 1984.

Coynik, David. *Film: Real to Reel.* Evanston, Illinois: McDougal-Littell,
   1976.

Ezmolian, John. *Lights! Camera! Scream! How to Make Your Own Monster
   Movie.* New York: Messner, 1983.

Hargrove, Jim. *Steven Spielberg: Amazing Filmmaker.* Chicago:
   Children's Press, 1988.

Schwartz, Perry. *Making Movies.* Minneapolis, Minnesota: Lerner, 1989.

Smith, Dian G. *American Filmmakers Today.* New York: Messner, 1983.

Smith, Dian G. *Great American Film Directors.* New York: Messner, 1987.

Staples, Terry. *Films and Videos.* New York: Warwick, 1986.

Tatchell, Judy and Cheryl Evans. *The Young Cartoonist.* Tulsa,
   Oklahoma: EDC, 1987.

Picture acknowledgments

Aardman Animation Ltd. 22 © Aardman Animation Ltd.; Aquarius 8 © Aquarius UK ; Joel Finler 7,
16 © Contemporary Films Ltd., 21 © Drawings by John Halas and Joy Batchelor; Ronald Grant
Archives 12, 14; John Halas 24 © *The Magic Lake* by Ivanov-Vano (USSR); Photri 11 (A. Novak), 13
(E.L. Drifmeyer); Topham 5 (both), 9, 17, 27; WPL/BFI stills cover © Universal City Studios, Inc., and
U-Drive Productions, Inc. All rights reserved. *An American Tail* and *An American Tail* logo are
trademarks of Universal City Studios, Inc. and U-Drive Productions, Inc. 4, 6, 10, 19 ©
Contemporary Films Ltd., 20; WPL 15, 25, 29; 26 © Pixar.

Index